For Mrs Barnett and Mrs Bettelley – B.M.

For Aunty Jilly, whose adventurous spirit and zest
for life will always inspire me – R.A.

First published in Great Britain in 2025 by Andersen Press Ltd.,
6 Coptic Street, London, WC1A 1NH, UK
Vijverlaan 48, 3062 HL Rotterdam, Nederland
 Printed and bound in China.
1 3 5 7 9 10 8 6 4 2
British Library Cataloguing in Publication Data available.
ISBN 978 1 83913 277 3

MIX
Paper | Supporting
responsible forestry
FSC® C104723

Great-Aunt Margot and Me

Bryher Mackenzie

Rhiannon Archard

ANDERSEN PRESS

Mondays are my favourite day.
A day for Great-Aunt Margot and me.
And when I visit Great-Aunt Margot on
Mondays after school . . .

She'll give me that look – the one
people say we share – and say those
words I just can't wait to hear,
"Pull up a chair, Pumpkin.
And, remind me . . . where were we?"

I get lots of things from
Great-Aunt Margot.

Like my love for
roller-skates,

shiny things,

library trips and
silliness.

Or the way we scream at the TV when our favourite team wins,

whisper to the plants and give them all names,

fancy the fanciest chocolates right before tea . . .

And can't help but dance when a band starts to sing.

I'm just like Great-Aunt Margot and Great-Aunt Margot is just like me.

Great-Aunt Margot has
been around forever.

She has lived
through wars and
storms, danced with
princesses and protestors

and travelled the
world by kayak and sled.

But lately . . .

Great-Aunt Margot seems to be forgetting lots of things (more things than usual anyway).

Like what day of the week it is

or the names of all
the plants I see.

She doesn't fancy screaming at football games or eating chocolates before tea.

She doesn't even feel like dancing and Great-Aunt Margot feels like dancing, always.

She says she doesn't feel the way she used to.
Like Great-Aunt Margot on
Mondays after school.

But when I look all around me, I see her memories everywhere, in everything. And an idea begins to tap-dance and shimmy into view.

I find all those shiny things and silly things and things that just scream: Great-Aunt Margot.

She is there:
In the posters and the placards,

magnets and
marbles,

pressed pennies, torn tickets

and the grooviest glasses
I've ever seen.

In the camper van that's
travelled far and is missing parts.
And the flag with all the colours
of the rainbow.
Great-Aunt Margot traces each
treasure with her fingers.

Her words dance around the living room as I listen to their stories, old and new.

Then her record player calls to me and
Great-Aunt Margot gives me that look.
That look I get from her, our twinkle.
As the sound of ***Scritch Scraaatch*** . . .

And a familiar song fills
the flat, Great-Aunt Margot
and I can't help but find our
groove as we

dance, dance, dance
on Mondays
after school.

Mondays
are my
favourite day.

Mondays are for
Great-Aunt Margot and me.